The animated film THE SNOWMAN™ AND THE SNOWDOG, produced in 2012,
is based on characters created by Raymond Briggs in the book *The Snowman,*
first published by Hamish Hamilton in 1978.
Licensed by Penguin Books Ltd.

Published in the United States by Random House Children's Books, a division
of Random House LLC, a Penguin Random House Company, New York.
Originally published in Great Britain by Penguin Books, London, in 2012.

Random House and the colophon are registered trademarks of Random House LLC.

thesnowman.com
Visit us on the Web! randomhouse.com/kids

Educators and librarians, for a variety of teaching tools,
visit us at RHTeachersLibrarians.com

Library of Congress Cataloging-in-Publication Data is available upon request.
ISBN 978-0-385-38714-9 (trade) — ISBN 978-0-385-38715-6 (ebook)

MANUFACTURED IN CHINA
10 9 8 7 6 5 4 3 2 1
First American Edition

Random House Children's Books supports the First Amendment and celebrates the right to read.

The Snowman™
AND THE SNOWDOG

based on characters created by
Raymond Briggs
and the story written by Hilary Audus and Joanna Harrison

Random House New York

“Come on,” called Billy to his dog.
“We’re here! Let’s explore our new home.”

But Billy's dog was too old and tired for exploring. As the months passed, he became slower and slower, and then one day he died.

Together Billy and his mom buried him in the yard.

Winter came. Billy was lonely.
He missed his old friend.

He had written a letter to Santa Claus and was about to take it downstairs when he tripped over a loose floorboard. . . .

"What's this?" thought Billy as he pulled out an old shoe box. Inside he found a worn-out hat, some coal, a shriveled tangerine, a tattered scarf . . .

. . . and an old photograph. In it, another boy stood outside Billy's new house next to an amazing snowman.

"I'll make a snowman too," thought Billy. "Just like his!"

He took the box outside

and began to build
his *own* snowman.

He used two pieces of coal for the eyes and
a new tangerine for the nose . . .

and, last of all, he gave him a great big
smile. His Snowman was perfect.

But there was still
plenty of snow left.

Billy started
building again . . .

and bit by bit, with two socks for ears, he made . . .

. . . a Snowdog!

By now, it was late. Billy said good night to his two new friends and went inside to bed.

At midnight, Billy was
woken by a muffled bark.

He peered out the window and rubbed his eyes
in disbelief. Did the Snowdog move?

Billy ran downstairs and
flung open the back door.
And then something
magical happened!

The Snowman and the Snowdog
came to life!

The Snowman politely shook
Billy's hand, and the Snowdog
bounded up to say hello.

Then the Snowdog ran through the backyard, where he found the old dog's ball. He wanted to play!

But the Snowman had found something too. It was a sled.

Billy climbed on board. Out through the gate they went, toward the park and up the hill.

When they reached the top,
Billy gasped in amazement.

The air was full of flying snowmen, rising up from the homes below. What a magical sight!

The Snowman took Billy's hand and started to run.
Billy grabbed the Snowdog, and before he knew it . . .

. . . they were **flying**!

They flew low over the rooftops,

then high above the city

and out across the countryside.

Just then, the Snowman
sneezed and his tangerine
nose blew off.

They swooped down to find it.
But instead, they found . . .
an airplane!

Together they went to take a closer look.

They climbed in, and with the Snowman at the controls, they were flying again.

Out to sea they flew, on and on toward the North Pole. . . .

When they arrived, they saw snowpeople everywhere!

They had come to compete in the

Snowman's Annual Downhill Race!

Billy and the Snowman reached the starting line just in time. The whistle blew and they were off!

Twisting and turning, they sped down the course. Soon Billy and the Snowdog were the only ones left, neck and neck with a penguin.

And just when it seemed the penguin would win, the Snowdog stretched forward and broke the finish-line tape with his nose!

They WON!

While they were celebrating,
Santa Claus arrived and
handed Billy a small parcel.
"This is for you.
Merry Christmas!"

But Billy had no time to open the parcel. . . .
Dawn was breaking and it was time to go.

When they landed in Billy's yard, it was time for him to go back inside to bed.

"I wish you could come with me," said Billy, "but you would melt indoors." Billy's eyes filled with tears.

He reached into his pocket for
a hankie and instead found the
present from Santa Claus.

Quickly he unwrapped it.
Inside was a brand-new dog
collar! He fastened it around
the Snowdog's neck.

"There," he said. "Just like a real dog!"

He turned to go, but as he did, the Snowdog's collar
started to glow, brighter and brighter, until . . .

“Woof!”
And where the Snowdog
had been was a real,
live dog, his tail wagging
with delight!

“Oh!” cried Billy. “You’re just what
I asked for in my letter to Santa!”

He hugged the Snowman with happiness.

Back in his bedroom,
Billy waved good night
to the Snowman.

Then he snuggled down in bed with his new friend.

"I think I'll call you Socks," he said
as he drifted off to sleep.

But when Billy woke up,
Socks was gone!
Had it all been a dream?

Hearing an excited bark, Billy rushed downstairs.
There was Socks, waiting to go outside and play!

Billy opened the door and out Socks sped,
bounding toward the Snowman. . . .

But the Snowman was gone,
melted away in the early-morning sun.